MAIRA KALMAN

DANIEL HANDLER

HURRY UP and WAIT

Series Editor
Sarah Hermanson Meister

The Museum of Modern Art
New York

Are you ready?

There are marks for you. Get on them.
Stand with your toes on the marks.

Then, get set.

We were looking at these pictures and
wondering what to do, and we said
to ourselves, what are they waiting for?
And what are we? Get going, get going.

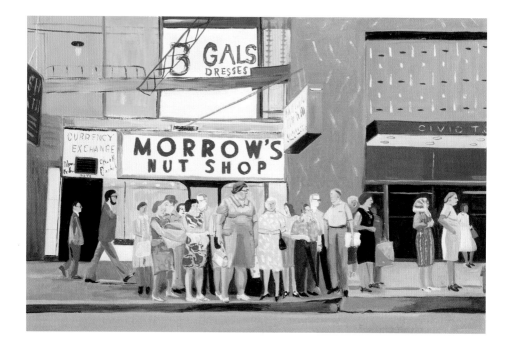

You're supposed to stop and smell the roses,
but truth be told it doesn't take that long
to smell them. You hardly have to stop.
You can smell the roses, and still have time to
run all those errands before the sun goes
down and it's dinner time.

If you go too fast you might not notice
everything. On the other hand, you don't want
to be late. So allow at least half an hour to do
everything. Minus sleeping and staring
out the window that's maybe ten things you
can do today, and you already woke up.

Somewhere in the world, always,
somebody is twenty minutes late for something,
and I am annoyed at them.

If you can't get there by yourself, someone might be able to take you. They might be going that way anyway, or more likely you will give them money and they'll do it.

This is the history of the entire world.

I was going to say something more about hurrying, but why take up your time? You have things to do. You can flip through this and go on to what it is that's waiting for you, the next thing.

And by *this* I mean everything.

All childhood long they told me to
hurry up, and now all this

Time

later I can't imagine what the rush was.
But every morning my child never puts on
his shoes on time, and we have to go,
we have to go.

When I was a kid my father would say,
if you get lost, don't look for me.
Stay there. Stay there and I will find you.

He's gone now.

We're talking about transportation, are we?
The way we go, quick or slow, one place
to another? Or are we talking about the fact
that we never go anywhere?

What time is it?

Some people, surely,
die on the way to something.

Then we call them the
late so-and-so.

If you had to leave right this
minute forever, what would you
take with you?

Just this. Just this.

Everything.

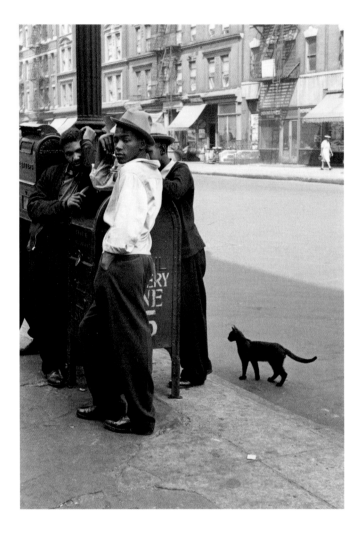

We look at these pictures and we find them
moving. We want to be moving, too.
But then sometimes we're tired of moving
and we want to wait for something else.

Jump right in, or wade in slowly.
Advantage to one, it's over quickly.
Advantage to the other, it isn't.

Next time, *you* hurry, and I'll be the thing
waiting here while you pass by.

It feels so good to go someplace.

Except when you want to stay
right there where you are.

I'm just standing still, and then suddenly
I think I am waiting for something.
Once I've decided I'm waiting it's like
I'm not standing still anymore.

Sometimes you will wait and wait.
So long, so patient you will be waiting.
You cannot stand it and still
you will wait. You will wait and wait
and then, finally—wait for it—

—nothing will happen.

Not worth waiting for. Yet here we are waiting for it.

I didn't even know I was waiting.
I thought I was just here.

The best thing you can say to me is,
let's get out of here.

Let's not go overboard, no, let's. Let's not go
too fast, no, let's. Let's not sit around waiting,
no, let's. These decisions are final.

Tell me exactly why I should go.

I mean, stay. Tell me that.

I see these pictures and wonder
where they've all gone to. I mean
they are still waiting right there,
but of course they've hurried on.

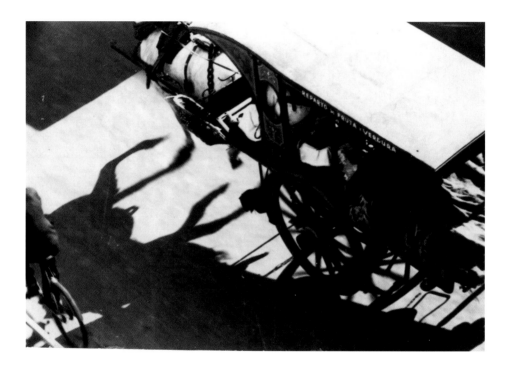

How long can we stay here?
We hurry around for a while
and then it's time to go.
Time to go. Everybody says it.
Time to go.

And then we do.

there is no such thing as waiting for daniel.
he is always ahead of me.

every time I have come around the corner
or into the lobby or into the room, there
he is waiting for me in a crisp shirt (pink?)
and an elegant suit (gray?).

once, only once, he was not, and I thought
that he must have fallen out of a window
or been hit by a bus. i went into a cold,
quiet panic.

and then daniel came walking around the
corner.

something insane had detained him.
it was not his fault at all. —M. K.

About the same time I met Maira, I made a New
Year's resolution never to run for a bus again. When
you run for a bus and miss it, you're humiliated.
When you run for a bus and catch it, you're on a bus.

I show up half an hour early for everything because
that's how I was raised. When I am meeting
Maira someplace I sit and wait but I don't mind. One
reason I don't mind is that I always have a book
with me. The other reason is that it's worth it. —D. H.

by the way, if you are in a hurry, the only
thing to do is slow down. —D. H. / M. K.

The book in your hands is similar to one called *Girls Standing on Lawns* in many significant ways. Both are collaborations between Maira Kalman, Daniel Handler, and The Museum of Modern Art. Both feature a sequence of photographs from MoMA's unparalleled collection, interspersed with Maira's tender and surprising paintings, and Daniel's evocative prose.

The books also match: both are eight inches tall, five inches wide, with identical letter styles (or typeface) and Maira's distinctive handwriting on the cover. But whereas *Girls Standing on Lawns* exclusively featured snapshots by photographers whose names are unknown to us, this book includes many photographs by photographers whose names we know, as well as a host of other details about what she or he thought, and why she or he made the work. In the museum world, we refer to this as the artist's intent, and we take it very seriously.

Curators are individuals who collect, preserve, and interpret objects, often those held by public institutions (the root of the word is *curare*, which in Latin means "to care for"). As a curator, I love to make connections between works of art, either by hanging them near one another in exhibitions or reproducing them next to one another in books. If I do this well, my audience learns something, or their curiosity is piqued, or, perhaps, they simply enjoy the art more deeply. But this is also a responsibility: by putting things together I'm implying there is a connection, and occasionally that connection would have been unimaginable to one or both of the artists (separated by generations, by oceans, or just by circles of acquaintances). So I do my best, in exhibitions and publications, to respect the artist's intent. Here, however, Maira and Daniel are using the works of art in a different way: they're making a work of art themselves (what we call an "artist's book"), so they aren't concerned if the makers of these photographs would have used the words "hurry" or "wait" to describe their images, or if they would have minded the implied connection to a work on the opposite page.

When one artist uses another artist's works as the basis for his or her own, it is something we refer to as "appropriation." You could say, for instance, that Maira appropriates a photograph when she uses it as the inspiration for one of her paintings. And all of the photographs take on new meaning in the context of Maira and Daniel's book. Some artists enjoy the potential for confusion and will deliberately say very little about what they think their work means, because they want us to come to our own conclusions. Some artists, such as El Lissitzky, whose design for a Soviet sports-club mural appears here, believed that art could change society. He so clearly declared his revolutionary intentions that I'm less comfortable using his image to tell a story about hurrying (even through he had no problem using the photographs of others as layers in his work). But we've included it anyway, to highlight this complication.

Sarah Hermanson Meister
Curator, Department of Photography
The Museum of Modern Art, New York

The Photographs

All works are in the collection of The Museum of Modern Art, New York.
Except where noted, they are gelatin silver prints. The dimensions correspond
to the image size with height preceding width.

Cover and page 1
Rudy Burckhardt
(American, born Switzerland.
1914–1999)
Untitled, from the
album *Photographs*
by Rudolph Burckhardt;
Sonnet by Edwin Denby.
1946–47. 10³⁄₁₆ × 7⁵⁄₁₆"
(25.8 × 18.6 cm). Gift
of CameraWorks, Inc.
and purchase

Page 5
Lee Friedlander
(American, born 1934)
New York City. 1962.
5¼ × 8" (13.3 × 20.3 cm).
Carl Jacobs Fund

Page 6
Michael Putnam
(American, born 1937)
New York City. 1970
(printed 2014). 7¹⁵⁄₁₆ ×
11⁷⁄₁₆" (20.1 × 29.1 cm).
Gift of the artist

Page 7
Jakob Tuggener
(Swiss, 1904–1988)
In the Morning. 1936.
15⁷⁄₈ × 11½" (40.3 ×
29.2 cm). Gift of the
artist

Page 8

Stephen Shore
(American, born 1947)
Chicago, Illinois. July
1972 (printed 2013).
Chromogenic color
print, 5 × 7½" (12.7 ×
19.1 cm). Gift of the
artist

Page 9
Tod Papageorge
(American, born 1940)
Fifth Avenue. 1970.
7¾ × 11¹¹⁄₁₆" (19.7 ×
29.7 cm). John
Parkinson III Fund

Page 10
Philip Fein
(American, 1912–1994)
Three Kids and a Sled.
c. 1940. 9⅛ × 10½"
(23.2 × 26.7 cm).
Purchase

Page 11
Philip-Lorca diCorcia
(American, born 1951)
Hong Kong. 1996.
Chromogenic color
print, 25⅜ × 37½"
(64.5 × 95.2 cm). Gift of
Carol and Arthur
Goldberg

Page 12
Unknown photographer
Untitled. c. 1930. 3¹⁄₁₆ ×
2¹⁄₁₆" (7.7 × 5.2 cm).
Gift of Peter J. Cohen

Page 14
Stephen Shore
(American, born 1947)
*Breakfast, Trail's End
Restaurant, Kanab,
Utah.* 1973. Chromo-
genic color print, 9 ×
11⅛" (22.9 × 28.3 cm).
Purchase

Page 15

Dorothea Lange
(American, 1895–1965)
*Man Stepping
from Cable Car, San
Francisco.* 1956. 9¾ ×
6⁷⁄₁₆" (24.8 × 16.4 cm).
Purchase

Page 16
Harry Callahan
(American, 1912–1999)
Chicago. 1950. 9³⁄₁₆ ×
13¹¹⁄₁₆" (23.3 × 34.8 cm).
Acquired with matching
funds from Shirley C.
Burden and the
National Endowment
for the Arts

Page 17
Garry Winogrand
(American, 1928–1984)
New York City. 1961.
13⅜ × 8⅞" (34 ×
22.5 cm). Gift of the
artist

Page 18
Helen Levitt
(American, 1913–2009)
New York. 1982. 9⁹⁄₁₆ ×
6⁷⁄₁₆" (24.3 × 16.4 cm).
Gift of Marvin Hoshino
in memory of
Ben Maddow

Page 19
Garry Winogrand
(American, 1928–1984)
New York City. 1968.
8⅞ × 13³⁄₁₆" (22.5 ×
33.5 cm). Purchase
and gift of Barbara
Schwartz in memory of
Eugene M. Schwartz

Page 20
Rudy Burckhardt
(American, born Switzerland.
1914–1999)
Untitled, from the
album *Photographs
by Rudolph Burckhardt;
Sonnet by Edwin Denby.*
1946–47. 7¹⁵⁄₁₆ × 11³⁄₁₆"
(20.2 × 28.4 cm). Gift
of CameraWorks, Inc.
and purchase

Page 21
Lee Friedlander
(American, born 1934)
New York City. 1963.
6⁷⁄₁₆ × 9⅝" (16.4 ×
24.5 cm). Purchase

Page 22
Dorothea Lange
(American, 1895–1965)
Mother and Child, San Francisco. 1952. 9⅜ × 7⁵⁄₁₆" (23.8 × 18.6 cm). Gift of the artist

Page 24
Judith Joy Ross
(American, born 1946)
Untitled, from *Eurana Park, Weatherly, Pennsylvania.* 1982. Gelatin silver printing-out-paper print, 9⅝ × 7¹¹⁄₁₆" (24.5 × 19.5 cm) Gift of Richard O. Rieger

Page 25

Helen Levitt
(American, 1913–2009)
Untitled, from *Projects: Helen Levitt in Color.* 1971–74. 35mm color slide. Purchase

Page 26
O. Winston Link
(American, 1914–2001)
Last Steam Locomotive Run on Norfolk and Western, Radford Division. December 31, 1957. 13½ × 10¹³⁄₁₆" (34.2 × 27.5 cm). Purchase

Page 27
Simpson Kalisher
(American, born 1926)
A Railroad Crossing. 1955. 4½ × 9¹⁄₁₆" (11.5 × 23 cm). Gift of Gloria Richards

Page 28
Eugène Atget
(French, 1857–1927)
Untitled [ragpicker]. 1899–1900. Gelatin silver printing-out-paper print, 8¹¹⁄₁₆ × 6⁹⁄₁₆" (22 × 16.7 cm). Abbott-Levy Collection. Partial gift of Shirley C. Burden

Page 29
Dorothea Lange
(American, 1895–1965)
On the Road to Los Angeles, California. 1937. 8 × 7¾" (20.4 × 19.7 cm). Gift of the Farm Security Administration

Page 30

Dora Maar
(French, born Russia. 1907–1997)
Untitled. c. 1935. 11¾ × 9³⁄₁₆" (29.8 × 23.4 cm). Robert and Joyce Menschel Fund

Page 31
Bill Brandt
(British, born Germany. 1904–1983)
Losing at the Horse Races, Auteuil, Paris. c. 1932. 8⅜ × 6¹⁵⁄₁₆" (21.3 × 17.6 cm). Gift of Edwynn Houk

Page 32
Helen Levitt
(American, 1913–2009)
New York. c. 1945 (printed c. 1970). 9¹³⁄₁₆ × 6¹³⁄₁₆" (24.9 × 17.2 cm). Gift of Janice Levitt

Page 33
Joel Sternfeld
(American, born 1944)
Summer Interns, Wall Street, New York. 1987. Chromogenic color print, 33¾ × 42½" (85.7 × 107.9 cm). Gift of the artist

Page 34

Henri Cartier-Bresson
(French, 1908–2004)
Behind the Gare St. Lazare. 1932 (printed c. 1950). 13⅞ × 9½" (35.2 × 24.1 cm). Gift of the artist, by exchange

Page 35

Times Wide World Photos
(American, active 1919–1941)
A Famous Fisherman in Action. 1932. 9⅝ × 7¾" (24.5 × 19.7 cm). The New York Times Collection

Page 37
Helen Levitt
(American, 1913–2009)
New York. 1983. 7¹⁄₁₆ × 10¾" (17.9 × 27.3 cm). Gift of Marvin Hoshino

Pages 38 and 39
Yves Klein
(French, 1928–1962)
Leap into the Void. 1960. Photograph by Shunk-Kender
(Harry Shunk [German, 1924–2006] and János Kender [Hungarian, 1937–1983]). 14³⁄₁₆ × 10¹³⁄₁₆" (36 × 27.4 cm). Gift of the Roy Lichtenstein Foundation in memory of Harry Shunk and János Kender

Page 40
Jacques-Henri Lartigue
(French, 1894–1986)
Paris, Avenue des Acacias. 1912 (printed 1962). 11¾ × 15½" (29.8 × 39.4 cm). Gift of the artist

Page 41
Jens S Jensen
(Swedish, born 1946)
Boy on the Wall, Hammarkullen, Gothenburg. 1973. 9⁷⁄₁₆ × 11¾" (24 × 29.8 cm). Gift of the artist

Page 42
Dora Maar
(French, born Russia. 1907–1997)
Untitled. c. 1930. 10⅜ x 9⅜" (26.4 x 23.9 cm). Horace W. Goldsmith Fund through Robert B. Menschel

Page 43

August Sander
(German, 1876–1964)
Young Girl in Circus Caravan. 1926. 11 × 8¹⁄₁₆" (27.9 × 20.4 cm). Gift of the artist

Page 45
Garry Winogrand
(American, 1928–1984)
Los Angeles Airport. 1964. 8¹⁵⁄₁₆ × 13¼" (22.7 × 33.7 cm). Purchase and gift of Barbara Schwartz in memory of Eugene M. Schwartz

Page 46

Walker Evans
(American, 1903–1975)
Subway Portrait. 1938–41. 7⁵⁄₁₆ × 7⅞" (18.6 × 20 cm). Purchase

Page 47
Brassaï
(French, born Transylvania. 1899–1984)
Couple Asleep in a Train. 1938. 9¼ × 11⁵⁄₁₆" (23.5 × 28.8 cm). Gift of Gilberte Brassaï

Page 48
Rosalind Fox Solomon
(American, born 1930)
Running Boy, Guatemala. 1978. 14¹⁵⁄₁₆ × 15" (37.9 × 38.2 cm). Gift of the artist

Page 49
Jacques-Henri Lartigue
(French, 1894–1986)
Grand Prix of the Automobile Club of France, Course at Dieppe. 1912 (printed 1962). 10 × 13½" (25.4 × 34.3 cm). Gift of the artist

Page 50
Times Wide World Photos
(American, active 1919–1941)
One of the Freak Hazards of the Road: A Motorcycle Sidecar. c. 1934. 5⁵⁄₁₆ × 7¼" (13.5 × 18.4 cm). The New York Times Collection

Page 51
Fred Hansen/Pacific and Atlantic Photos
(American, active 1921–1932)
Just Before the Waves Closed Over the Vestris. November 12, 1928. 9¼ × 7³⁄₁₆" (23.5 × 18.2 cm). The New York Times Collection

Pages 52–53
Eadweard J. Muybridge
(American, born England. 1830–1904)
Woman Jumping, Running Straight High Jump, from *Animal Locomotion.* 1884–86. Collotype, 7³⁄₁₆ × 16⅞" (18.3 × 42.9 cm). Gift of the Philadelphia Commercial Museum

Page 54
Horacio Coppola
(Argentine, 1906–2012)
Buenos Aires. 1931. 3⅛ × 4⁹⁄₁₆" (8 × 11.6 cm). Vital Projects Fund, Robert B. Menschel

Page 58
El Lissitzky
(Russian, 1890–1941)
Runner in the City. 1926. 10½ × 8¹³⁄₁₆" (26.7 × 22.4 cm). Thomas Walther Collection. Gift of Thomas Walther

Page 63
Friedrich Seidenstücker
(German, 1882–1966)
Puddle Jumper. 1925. 7⅛ × 5⅛" (18.1 × 13 cm). Thomas Walther Collection. Abbott-Levy Collection funds, by exchange

Back cover
Bill Rauhauser
(American, born 1918)
Three on a Bench, Detroit River. c. 1952. 15⁷⁄₁₆ × 19⁵⁄₁₆" (39.2 × 49 cm). Gift of the artist

Credits

Support for this publication was provided
by the Nancy Lee and Perry Bass Publication
Endowment Fund.

Produced by the Department of Publications
The Museum of Modern Art, New York
Christopher Hudson, Publisher
Chul R. Kim, Associate Publisher
David Frankel, Editorial Director
Marc Sapir, Production Director

Edited by Chul R. Kim and Emily Hall
Designed by Beverly Joel, pulp, ink.
Production by Marc Sapir
Photograph research by Tasha Lutek
Permissions and clearances by Makiko Wholey
Printed and bound by Trifolio, Verona, Italy

This book is typeset in Avenir and Sentinel.
The paper is 150 gsm Magno Plus matte.

Library of Congress Control Number: 2014955434
ISBN: 978-0-87070-959-3

Distributed in English by Abrams Books for
Young Readers, an imprint of ABRAMS, New York

Printed in Italy

The authors would like to extend a special thanks
to Peter J. Cohen, for his ongoing support of
this series, and to the artists whose photographs
appear on these pages.